Postman Pat
and the
Dinosaur Bone

Story by **John Cunliffe**
Pictures by **Joan Hickson**

From the original Television designs by **Ivor Wood**

André Deutsch/Hippo Books

Published simultaneously in hardback by
André Deutsch Limited
105-106 Great Russell Street, London WC1B 3LJ
and in paperback by Hippo Books, Scholastic Publications Limited,
10 Earlham Street, London WC2H 9RX in 1988
Second impression 1988
Third impression 1989
Text copyright © 1988 by John Cunliffe
Illustrations copyright © 1988 by André Deutsch Limited
Scholastic Publications Limited
and Woodland Animations Limited

ISBN 0 233 98282 5 (hardback)
ISBN 0 590 70933 X (paperback)

Made and printed in Belgium by Proost

It was a fine April morning. Peter
Fogg was out early, ploughing the top
field. Pat gave him a wave as he went
by.

Pat's first call was at Greendale School. The children were busy. Katy and Tom were painting a picture. They were painting it on the biggest piece of paper they could find, spread out on the floor. It was too big for the table.

"What on earth is that?" said Pat.

"It's a dinosaur," said Tom. "A diplo . . . something."

"A diplodocus," said Katy.

"Ugh," said Pat, "I wouldn't like to meet him on a dark night. I hope there are no letters for him. Let's see . . . no, there's nothing for anyone called diplo. . .whatsit, today."

"Diplodocus," said Katy, "can't you remember?"

"He eats postmen," said Tom.

"Nasty," said Pat. "Worse than Captain Forbes' dog. He tries to eat postmen, but he's not as big as that fellow."

"They didn't have postmen when he was alive," said Bill Thompson.

"Hello, Bill," said Pat. "What are you doing? My, that's good! It looks even worse."

Bill was making a model.

"It's a flying dinosaur," said Bill.

"Well, I never," said Pat.

"But they all died a long time ago," said Bill. "Before there were any postmen, or any people at all."

"So how do you know what they looked like?" said Pat.

"Bones," said Bill.

"Bones?"

"They dig them up. Fossils. Bones turned into stone."

"Bless us," said Pat. "I'd better get on with these letters."

When Pat called at the church, he told the Reverend Timms about the dinosaurs.

"Ah, yes, Pat," said the Reverend. "Our ancient forbears."

"Not bears, Reverend," said Pat.

"Worse than bears. Great golloping monsters that lived here, in Greendale."

"The beasts that came before us," said the Reverend. "And they weren't all big, you know. I have a fossil in the garden."

"Help!" said Pat.

"He doesn't bite," said the Reverend.
"Come and see."
They went into the garden, and the
Reverend Timms showed Pat a stone in
the rockery. There was a shape in the
stone. It looked like a curly shell.
"Well, I never!" said Pat.

Pat had three letters for Granny Dryden. She was hanging the washing out. He told her about the dinosaurs. "It must have been a long time ago," she said. "There were none when I was a girl. It was all sums and needlework. And we had enough to do, looking after the sheep and cows. Pass the pegs, please. Dinosaurs, indeed!"

There was a parcel for Ted Glen. He was busy putting a new silencer on the Landrover.

"Could you put the parcel on the bench, please?" he asked. "I can't let go of this nut."

Pat looked round Ted's garden.
"You haven't got any dinosaur bones
in your garden, have you?" he said.
"They could do with some at the school."
Jess came to have a look.

But he was looking for mice in the
hedge.
"I think Jess would have found them
long ago," said Ted.

There was a magazine, two letters and
a card for Miss Hubbard. She was
busy spring cleaning. Pat told her
about the dinosaurs.

"Pass that duster, please," she said. "I had an aunt who found a fossil once. She sold it to a museum for twenty pounds. It was a lot of money in those days."

"Money for old bones," said Pat.

When Pat had delivered all his letters, he passed Peter Fogg again, on the way back. Peter had stopped his tractor, and he was looking at something the plough had dug up. Pat stopped to have a look.

"What have you found, Peter?" he said.

"It's a bone," said Peter.

"A bone?" said Pat. "Let's have a look. It might be a dinosaur bone."

"A what-er-sore?" said Peter.

"A dinosaur," said Pat. And he told them about Katy and Tom's picture, and Bill's model.

"Oh, I see," said Peter. "I once did a project on that at school. Well, you never know. It does look a funny sort of bone. But it might just be an old sheep bone."

"It looks like a dinosaur bone to me," said Pat.

"Why don't you take it to Pencaster museum," said Peter. "They'll tell you."

So Pat put the bone in his van. Jess didn't like it at all. He put his claws out when he saw it.

"It's all right," said Pat. "It won't hurt you."

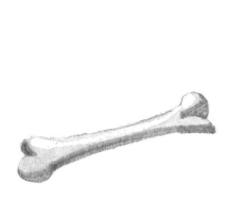

But Jess sat as far away from it as he
could, and watched it all the way
home.

Pat got his bike out, and put the bone
in the saddlebag, and rode into
Pencaster that very afternoon.

There was a class of children from
Kendal, looking at the old water-wheel,
and Pat had to wait while Mr. Ruston
told them all about it.

When Mr. Ruston saw the bone,
he began to laugh.

"Oh, dear, Pat. That's no dinosaur
bone! It's the leg bone of a cow! I'm
afraid you've had a wasted trip."

Pat smiled.

"Well, no, it's not a waste," he said.
"I've learnt something, haven't I, even
if I do feel a bit silly."

"No, it's not silly to find things out, Pat," said Mr. Ruston, kindly. "But you can learn something more. Come this way, and I'll show you whilst the children are busy drawing the water-wheel."

Mr. Ruston took Pat to another room in the museum. There was a whole case, full of dinosaur bones.

"The real thing," said Mr. Ruston. "Collected by Captain Hargreaves a hundred years ago."

'I bet the children would like to see hese," said Pat.

"Then bring them," said Mr. Ruston.

"I'll have a word with Mr. Pringle," said Pat.

The very next day, Pat told the whole story to Mr. Pringle and the children at Greendale school.

"Wonderful!" said Mr. Pringle. "Just what we need for our project."

"I'll have a word with Ted," said Pat, "and see if he can take you in his bus."

It was all fixed up in a week. Mr. Pringle closed the school, and they took a picnic and made a day of it. It was a lovely day. The children drew the bones, and Mr. Ruston took them out of the case, and said they could hold them if they were very careful. "Ace!" said Bill.

When they had seen everything at the museum, they climbed up the hill to Pencaster castle, and ate their sandwiches in the sun.